THE MYSTERY OF THE MAGIC GREEN BALL

THE MYSTERY
OF THE
MAGIC GREEN BALL

STORY AND PICTURES BY Steven Kellogg

The Dial Press / New York

a pied piper book

FOR TREMAINE

My big brother Albert gave me this green ball. The T stands for Timmy.

That's me.

I shared it with my friend Peggy. I let all of Albert's friends play with it too.

Except for Sara Bianco. I never even showed it to her because she wouldn't let me touch her new magic set.

One day Louis Smith hit my ball into the woods.

"We'll never find it," said Albert. "It's the same color as the leaves."

Louis said, "Let's give up."

"Not me!" I said. "I'll never give up!" Peggy said she wouldn't either.

Albert said, "Wait until the leaves turn brown in the fall. It'll be easy to find."

The next day Sara came over with her magic set.
Peggy and I said, "Teach us some magic tricks."

Sara said, "Nobody touches this magic set but me."

So Peggy and I went to look for the lost green ball.

During the fall Sara came over almost every day after school to practice her magic tricks.

I said, "I sure wish I could be a magician."

She said, "I'm the only magician in this neighborhood."

Albert was wrong about how easy it would be to spot my green ball in the brown leaves.

It wasn't easy to find in the snow either.

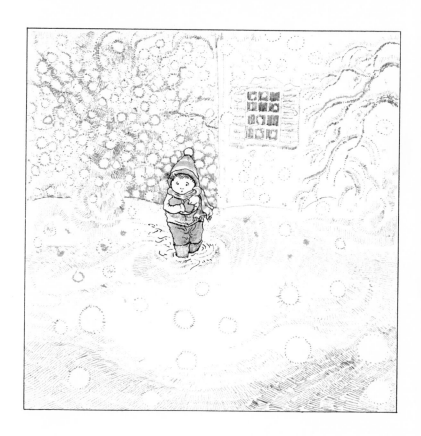

Once, several months later, we thought we'd spotted it.

But it was only the first green leaf of spring.

On Saturday Albert told me that the people on the next street were having a neighborhood carnival.

When I got there, Josey Wiggins said the Mystery Gypsy Fortune Teller had told her that someday she would be president of the moon.

And she told Louis Smith that he was going to marry a two-thousand-pound gorilla.
I got in line.

When it was my turn, I paid the Mystery Gypsy and said,
"Once I lost something, and I never found it again."

She said, "Tell me what you lost, little boy. The answers to all mysteries are here in my magic green ball."

I said, "That ball is what I'm looking for! It's mine."

The Mystery Gypsy said, "I found this ball! It's mine, and nobody touches it but me!"

I could tell by the way the Mystery Gypsy yelled that she was really Sara Bianco. She threw me out of the tent.

I went home and telephoned Peggy.

She promised to help me get my ball back.

A few minutes later she arrived with a grapefruit.

We painted it so it looked just like my ball.

Then we took it to the carnival in a paper bag.

Peggy started kicking the Mystery Gypsy's tent while
I ran behind it.

Sara Bianco came out yelling.

While she was outside the tent, I slipped in the back and exchanged the grapefruit for my green ball.

When the Mystery Gypsy discovers her magic green grapefruit, she'll know she's not the only magician in this neighborhood.